MW01054958

With love to my parents, Paul and Mary Anne Jennette,
who took me everywhere.

—JMC

To Rosie, Paul, Lynn, Donna, Jamie and Debi,
thank you for all your love, support and encouragement.

— LMG

Text copyright Jean M. Cochran © 2008
Illustrations copyright Lee M. Gullens © 2008

ISBN: 978-0-9792035-1-0
Library of Congress Control Number: 2007933793

10 9 8 7 6 5 4 3 2 1
Printed and bound in the USA

Published by Pleasant St. Press
PO Box 520
Raynham Center, MA 02768 USA

www.pleasantstpress.com
e-mail: info@pleasantstpress.com

Book Design & Layout by Jill Ronsley
suneditwrite.com

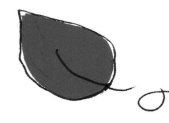

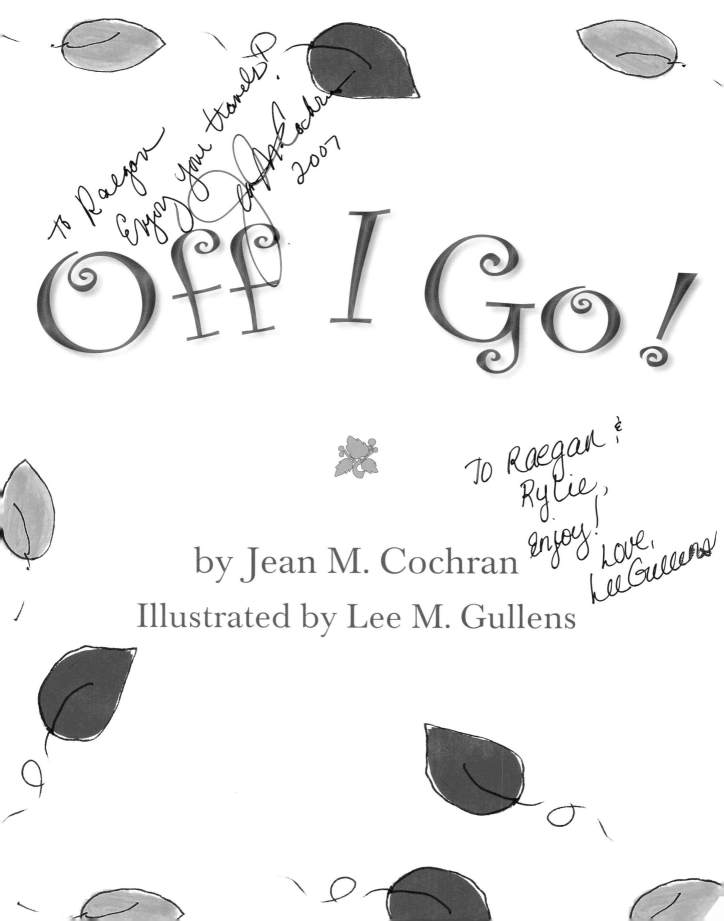

Off I Go!

To Raegan
Enjoy your travels!
[signature] 2007

by Jean M. Cochran

To Raegan &
Rylie,
enjoy!
Love,
Lee Gullens

Illustrated by Lee M. Gullens

Hats up high. Boots down low.
Zip my jacket. Off I go!

Out the door and down the street,
Skipping on my dancing feet.

Down the hill I hop, hop, hop.
Crossing guard says, "Stop! Stop! Stop!"

Dump truck hauls its heavy load.
Bumping, thumping down the road.

Cross the bridge, way up high.
Busy cars are whizzing by.

See the people down below.
Waving, waving ... Say, "Hello!"

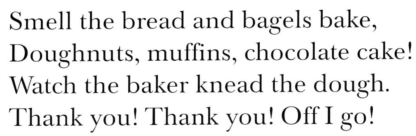

Smell the bread and bagels bake,
Doughnuts, muffins, chocolate cake!
Watch the baker knead the dough.
Thank you! Thank you! Off I go!

Through the puddles, run and romp.
Splishing, splashing, skip and stomp.
Ducklings swimming in a row.
Paddle, paddle! Off they go!

Tippy-toes can reach the trees.
Swing me higher in the breeze.
Climb the ladder. Watch me glide.
Faster, faster down the slide.

Shhh! Be quiet! Baby's resting,
Under blankets softly nestling.

Cherry mouth and rosy cheek.
Gently, gently–take a peek.

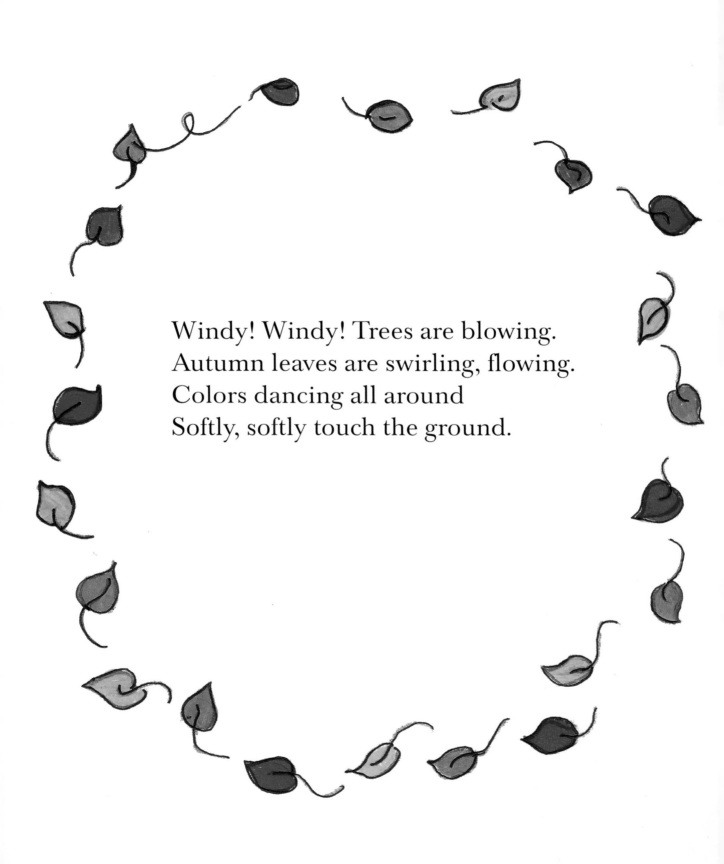

Windy! Windy! Trees are blowing.
Autumn leaves are swirling, flowing.
Colors dancing all around
Softly, softly touch the ground.

Marching, marching through the town.
Busy people all around.
Red lights flash and sirens blow.
Hurry! Hurry! Off they go!

Up the hill and down the street,
Step by step on weary feet,
Slowly, slowly home I go.
Hats up high. Boots down low.

Hang my jacket on the hook.
Cozy, cozy ... read a book.

Climb into a comfy lap.
Nuzzle, cuddle ... time to nap.

Softly sing a dreamy song.
Sweetly, sweetly sing along.
Rocking gently to and fro,
Sleepy, sleepy ...

Off ... I ... go ...